Haddy the Doorstopasaurus

New Jersey's First Dinosaur Find

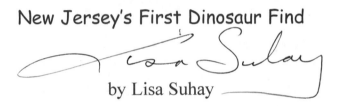

by Lisa Suhay

Twenty-five cents from the sale of each book will benefit H.A.T.C.H.
Haddonfield Acts To Create Hadrosaurus

For more information, visit

www.hadrosaurus.com

www.franklinmasonpress.com

Franklin Mason Press   Trenton, New Jersey

This book is dedicated to those in Haddonfield, New Jersey and elsewhere who keep the history of the Hadrosaurus discovery alive.

And to my crew of explorers, artists and poets: sons, Zoltan, Ian, Avery and my husband, Robert.

Special thanks to Kris Wells and Mitchell L. Blumenthal at the New York Times, because, when they thought of dinosaurs they thought of me.   ....LS

Franklin Mason Press ISBN 0-9679227-8-X
Library Of Congress Control Number 2003112514

Text Copyright ©2003 by Lisa Suhay
Cover Design: Peri Poloni www.knockoutbooks.com

Editorial Staff: Marcia Jacobs, Brooks Spencer, Linda Funari

www.franklinmasonpress.com

Contents

Chapter One

"This is boring," Zoltan groaned as he stared down at the blank page in his writing journal.

At age nine he was tall and strong, with short, blond hair, blue eyes and a very serious frown. While he had a good sense of humor and liked to have fun, he was deadly serious when it came to homework and anything to do with school.

Zoltan Magyar was the oldest of three boys. Being the oldest meant that he was the first to do everything. He was the first to do well and the first to make mistakes at new things.

Even his name was the first one in his family to be really different. His father chose the name because their family heritage was Hungarian. In Hungarian, the name MAGYAR means "from Hungary." It's like saying "I'm an American." When Zoltan's great-great-grandparents had arrived at Ellis Island the customs officer asked, "O.K. Mack, what's your name?" The officer called everybody Mack.

Since they didn't speak any English, Zoltan's great-great-grandfather had pointed to himself and said, "Magyar." He was trying to say that he was from Hungary. The customs man had written "Name: Mack Magyar."

Zoltan always wondered if he were to move to Hungary would his name be changed to "Mack American" by somebody who didn't understand him.

Since then every first-born son in their family had been named Mack Magyar and Zoltan's dad decided it was time for it to stop. He wanted his son to have a real Hungarian name. He chose the name of his favorite Hungarian Composer, Zoltan Kodaly, who lived from 1882 until 1967.

Zoltan hated being first. He was terribly shy. He hated being the first to try new things because he believed that if he failed he was the first to fail and that made it worse. Even though he was good at almost everything he tried, he worried just the same.

He hated making mistakes or doing anything wrong because he always felt as if everyone was watching him and waiting to see how he did everything. When it came to his younger brother Ian, Zoltan was absolutely right about always being watched.

"What's boring," Ian asked, adjusting his eyeglasses on his nose and looking hard at his older brother.

Ian was skinny with shiny brown hair and green eyes behind gold-rimmed eyeglasses. He was always trying to be the best at everything too. He watched Zoltan like a hawk. Any tiny scrap of information he could get out of his older brother was like a prize.

Zoltan was nine and in third grade, while Ian was eight and in second.

Ian was keenly interested in Zoltan's homework assignments. He figured he was getting secret, inside information on what he would have to do next year.

Right at this moment, he was worried because he was certain that

Zoltan groaning and saying something was "boring" were very bad signs.

"I have this assignment for next week, to write a poem," Zoltan said. The way he said it you could tell he thought this was just about the worst thing Mrs. Warner could possibly have asked him to do. "A long poem. It has to fill two entire pages!"

Ian wasn't sure this was so terrible. "So what's the problem?"

Zoltan rolled his eyes. For some people writing was an easy thing, but for him it was torture. How was he supposed to think of an idea?

Besides, he was great at math and science and they didn't need words, just numbers and discoveries.

Zoltan was sure nobody ever wrote poems about science, space or anything interesting. Poetry and science just didn't go together. Poems were sappy and boring, while science was awesome and powerful.

"The problem is that it's boring! I can't think of anything to write about," Zoltan said as he snapped his pencil in half. "And besides, poems are always about stuff like kissing and flowers."

Ian fell over in a fit of giggles.

"What?" Zoltan demanded. "What's so funny?"

More giggles. Ian was rolling around on the dining room floor with his bare feet in the air.

Zoltan shook his head in disgust. Little brothers were such a pain!

"Kissing flowers!" Ian gasped between laughs.

"That's NOT what I said," Zoltan shouted turning red in the face. "I did not say KISSING FLOWERS...I said..."

"Who's kissing flowers?" their

mother interrupted as she walked into the dining room. The boys always did their homework on the big wooden table under the big overhead light.

"Mom!" Zoltan said glaring at Ian. "Nobody's kissing anything! I have this stupid, stupid, boring poem to write."

"Well if that's the problem, then don't write a stupid, stupid, boring one. Write a smart, smart, interesting one," mom said as if that settled the matter. Zoltan glared. He was getting completely frustrated by all this silly talk.

"Mom!" Zoltan cried. "This is serious. I have two whole pages of stupid poem to write and no idea what to do. I only have two days and even if I had two years I couldn't do this!"

Besides, he thought, it was the middle of winter, snowing and there weren't even any stupid flowers to write about.

Mom said, "Poems don't have to be about flowers, but they are kind of like them. The idea for a poem starts small, like a seed, and then it takes time to grow and bloom in your mind."

Ian, who was sitting on the floor behind his mother, made a face like someone who was going to be sick and stuck out his tongue.

Zoltan smirked. Mom whipped around and caught Ian just as he had both his hands around his own neck, pretending to choke.

Mom grabbed him and began to tickle. While Ian giggled she recited:

"There was a boy named Ian
who made a face,
thinking Mom wouldn't see him.
She turned around
and in one bound
she had him in her grip.
She tackled
and tickled
Ian giggled
And rolled on the floor.
Then he didn't make that face
anymore!"

Mom stopped tickling and Ian stopped giggling.

Zoltan stared at his mother. "Man! I wish I could do my poem that fast," he complained.

"Not every poem is a quick rhyme," she said. "Sometimes it just takes time."

"Hey, rhyme, time, you did it again," Ian said. "Cool. You should be in school."

"Hey! I did it too, Zoltan!" Ian said with a grin.

This did not help Zoltan at all because now he felt as if anyone could write a poem easier than he could. He was never going to be able to do this stupid, stupid assignment. He frowned and slammed his composition book closed on the table with a thwump!

"Maybe you should do your other homework first and then take a break to think about the poem problem," his mother said. "It's Friday and it isn't due until Monday. So take a breather."

This was by far the best idea Zoltan had heard yet. Anything to get away from the Poem of Doom.

His other homework was going to be a snap because it was about dinosaurs. Now that was something interesting. Learning about giant lizards that roamed in strange and exotic places a million years ago was awesome.

Zoltan's favorite dinosaur was the tyrannosaurus rex because a T-Rex was big and strong. Right now it was his favorite because he was picturing how wonderful it would be if a T-Rex came stomping through his yard, into his house and ate his journal book.

Aaaaaaaaaaah, now that would be beautiful.

Zoltan was sure that there had never been any dinosaurs in New Jersey, especially not way down in the southern part of the state where they lived in the little town of Haddonfield.

New Jersey was dull. It was full of highways and schools and teachers who wanted you to write stupid, boring poems. No self-respecting giant lizard would be caught dead here.

As he looked through the pages of his science book and saw the pictures of New Mexico where the massive bones of the dinosaurs were being found he wished with all his heart that he lived there.

"Man," he said to Ian. "Look at this picture of New Mexico. Check out that desert and all that orange sand and those huge canyons."

Ian leaned over the book. He saw the pictures of the paleontologists, scientists who study the remains of creatures that died millions of years ago then hardened into rock-like things called fossils. Ian had a real fossil in his room. It was the imprint of a leaf left in the mud that had gotten hard and turned into rock. It was his prize possession and he knew that having it made Zoltan really jealous.

One picture in the book showed a team of paleontologists working in the hot sun to unearth the bones of a dinosaur. There were also pictures of fossils.

In another picture it showed how the bones, almost a whole skeleton, were all laid out on the ground in the shape of a dinosaur.

"Can you imagine finding just one of those bones," Ian said in wonder. "As soon as the snow melts I'm going to dig in the yard and see if I can find one."

Zoltan looked at his younger brother as if he were the dumbest person on the planet. He shook his head and said, "Don't be ridiculous. You would never, ever, find a dinosaur bone in New Jersey."

But the idea of digging for real dino bones gave him an idea and so he asked his mother. "Mom, can we move to New Mexico?"

"Sure, right after dinner," mom said.

"Mom! I'm serious," Zoltan said. "New Jersey is boring. All the dinosaurs came from New Mexico. Can we at least go visit there and see where the dinosaurs lived?"

Mom stopped cooking and looked at him. She raised her eyebrows. "You want to go see where dinosaurs used to live?" she asked. "I think that can be arranged."

"Yippee," Ian shouted. "We're moving to New Mexico!"

"I don't think I said that," Mom laughed. "But if you want to walk around someplace where dinosaurs used to roam we can definitely accommodate you."

Both boys looked confused and a little suspicious. They knew when either of their parents got that funny look that something was going to go wrong.

"I don't mean a trip to the museum," Zoltan said knowingly. After all, he was nine now and much too smart to fall for one of his mother's tricks.

"Neither do I," she said. "Are you both done with your homework?"

"Yes," Zoltan said. "Don't change the subject. We want to go to New Mexico."

"Right," Mom said. "First, I'd like for you two to do me a favor. Mr. Giannotti needs some help at his house and I think you two are perfect for the job."

Oh no! This was a nightmare. Mom was not only changing the subject, she was sending them off to be slave labor for the sculptor who lived down the road on West End Avenue.

Zoltan and Ian liked the statues Mr. Giannotti made and thought his studio was really awesome. But the last thing they wanted to do was work.

They were so close to convincing Mom to go to dinotopia and now this!

"But mom!" they both whined together.

"And don't call me Butt Mom," their mother joked. "Go. The fresh air and a little exercise will do you both good."

Things having gone from bad to worse, the boys pulled on their heavy coats and boots and headed off to Mr. Giannotti's house.

Chapter Two

As the two brothers trudged up the snowy lane to Mr. Giannotti's house Ian complained bitterly.

"I can't believe you got us stuck doing this," Ian griped. "We could be playing. Now we're probably going to have to shovel snow, or carry in firewood or something horrible!"

Zoltan didn't say anything. He just stomped along, occasionally kicking aside hunks of ice that had the misfortune of getting in his way.

As they got close enough to see the sculptor's house up ahead they saw a big pick-up truck out front by the curb.

A man in a red and black-checkered coat with a fluffy fur hat was unloading what looked like giant gray bricks.

When they got right up behind him he turned and they saw that it was Mr. Giannotti.

"Oh boys, I am really glad to see you!"

He dropped the big gray block he

was holding and it landed squarely on his big toe. He hopped around and made woofing sounds for a minute.

"Hoo boy is that clay heavy," he groaned. "Did you come to help me carry it into the studio?"

The boys looked at each other and shrugged their shoulders. Why not? They nodded "yes" and began to help haul the blocks from the truck to the gate and up the path to the big old barn of a studio.

"PHEW! This big boy's going to need tons of clay before I'm done," Mr. Giannotti said. "And that's just to make the sculpture that will become the mold for the bronze casting that will be the final statue. I really have a huge job ahead of me."

Zoltan looked up and saw a huge wire skeleton of a life-sized dinosaur! He knew Mom had been up to something. She must have known about this dinosaur all along. But that still wasn't as good as actually going to a place where real live dinosaurs had once lived.

If Mom thought she was going to get away that easily she was sadly mistaken.

"Whoa!" Ian said when he too looked up and saw the wire dino looming high above them. "That's wicked!"

Mr. Giannotti laughed. "Actually, this fellow here wasn't wicked at all. The hadrosaurus (HAD-ROW-SORE-US) foulkii (FOLK-EE) dinosaur was an herbivore, which means it only ate plants. No other dinos on the menu."

"No, I mean wicked in a good way. Like cool," Ian said.

"Oh, I see," the sculptor nodded. "Well, in any case, this hadrosaurus was a friendly dinosaur. A duck-billed type and a very famous one, too."

Zoltan walked up to it and saw where the sculptor had begun to put clay onto the wire frame, like flesh on a skeleton. On other visits to the studio

Mr. Giannotti had shown him and Ian how sculptures begin with the wire and then the clay is added.

When the clay sculpture is completed then a plaster mold is made from it. Mr. Giannotti would then heat up a metal called bronze that would get poured into the mold. When the liquid metal cooled off it would be a solid metal sculpture that looked exactly like the clay one but that would last and last.

"Where's this one going," Zoltan asked.

He knew that one of the other sculptures made by Mr. Giannotti, of a very famous writer named Walt

Whitman, was at the Camden, New Jersey Aquarium in the Children's Gardens. The boys were always very impressed that their very own neighbor had made something that everybody visited.

"Is it going to Japan like that one you made that time," Ian asked eagerly. "Or England or New York City or Florida like the others?"

The sculptor shook his head and patted the wire dino with his strong hand.

"Nope, guess again."

The boys looked at each other

and called out other exotic destinations including: "New Mexico?"

"Nope, again," he said. "This one's staying right here in Haddonfield. It will be right on Lantern Lane in the center of town. The Garden Club and people in town raised the money and asked me to make it. All two tons of history and glory right here for all of us to keep."

"Whoa," Ian gasped in appreciation. "That's really wicked."

Mr. Giannotti squinted at the dinosaur and then back at Ian. He still didn't quite understand that "wicked" was a good thing where Ian and other kids were concerned.

"Can you tell us anything else about the hadrosaurus?" Zoltan asked.

So the sculptor sat himself down on a big block of clay and explained that the hadrosaurus lived during a time called the Cretaceous period - roughly 84 to 71 million years ago. Back then Haddonfield was under 100 feet of sea water.

"This place was under the ocean," Zoltan asked in amazement. This visit was turning out to be a much better idea than he had thought it would.

"Oh yes," the sculptor said. "The beach wasn't way over on Long Beach

Island, an hour away like it is now. No. Back then it was just west of here in Philadelphia."

"Whoa," Ian gasped. "Wicked."

The sculptor winked at Ian and continued.

"Anyway, that's where all the marl pits come from," he said.

"Um, what's marl?" Ian asked.

Mr. Giannotti explained that marl is a kind of crumbly soil, rich in nutrients (vitamins for plants) and ancient sea life.

"People around here would dig up the marl and sell it to people to use in their gardens as fertilizer."

Zoltan remembered a story his father told him once about their Great, Great, Uncle Carl who was a wonderful gardener and how he had used marl in his garden.

In fact, Great-Great-Uncle Carl had worked in the marl pit, which was once owned by a farmer named John E. Hopkins. Farmer Hopkins' place was just a few houses away from Mr. Giannotti's house on West End Avenue.

All that was very interesting, but Zoltan still thought it would be more fun to go to New Mexico and see where dinosaurs had ruled the earth.

Zoltan wondered how many bites it would take a T-Rex to eat a hadrosaurus.

"That's interesting. But I like the T-Rex best," he said to the sculptor. "You should do one of those next time."

The sculptor nodded. "You know why I chose this particular dinosaur to turn into a sculpture?"

The boys shook their heads, no.

"No idea at all?"

They shook their heads harder.

Mr. Giannotti got to his feet and dragged over two large blocks of clay that were wrapped tightly in plastic and told the boys to have a seat. The boys sat on the squashy seats. Mr. Giannotti stood up to lecture like their teachers at Taunton Forge School often did.

Ian was having trouble paying attention. Instead he giggled to himself as he imagined leaving a print of his behind in the clay when he got up.

The artist smiled knowingly, "I will treasure your behind print forever Ian. I promise to use that block to make Haddy's rump!"

"Who's Haddy?" Ian asked.

"That's just my little pet name for the hadrosaurus I'm making. I call him Haddy for short."

"I'm making a hadrosaurus because the town of Haddonfield is having a big celebration to mark the day 145 years ago when the world's first nearly complete dinosaur skeleton was found right here in our very own marl pit," he said.

There was complete silence. And then: "What? Here? A dinosaur lived here?" Zoltan asked.

"Wicked," said Ian.

It was Mr. Giannotti's turn to laugh. "Oh Ian, we really have to get you a new word."

"Yes, the hadrosaurus was dis-covered right here in farmer Hopkins' marl pit just down the street in the big ravine."

The ravine was in a wooded area just at the very edge of the big public park. It was a steep place that led down to a very ancient stream.

Zoltan looked up at the wire skeleton and then back at the sculptor. He was thinking, "This can't be right."

Out loud he said, "Dinosaurs don't come from New Jersey. They come from New Mexico. I read it in my science book." He added, "Nothing cool comes from New Jersey!"

"You came from New Jersey," the sculptor pointed out. That brought a new silence as Zoltan thought about it and Ian struggled against a fresh wave of giggles.

Now Mr. Giannotti raised an eyebrow and shook his head. He knew how the boys felt. He had grown up in the town himself and knew all too well how hard it was to believe that this sleepy little place could be associated with anything so amazing as a giant lizard.

Mr. Giannotti went over to a large cabinet where he kept all his research and books.

When a sculptor sets out to create anything as complicated as a dinosaur he needs to do lots of studying to be certain it is as true to the real thing as possible.

To Mr. Giannotti's way of thinking, nothing would be more embarrassing than making a mistake on a two ton bronze dinosaur that would sit in the center of town, right on Lantern Lane for the whole world to see!

He explained this to the boys as he set up book after book and page after page of pictures and scientific stories about their very own Haddonfield Hadrosaurus foulkii.

"Boys, this here is the most famous dinosaur in the world," he explained.

Zoltan found this very hard to believe and he said so.

But the sculptor was not the least bit insulted or surprised.

"This dinosaur is not only famous, it's funny," he continued.

He explained that for years the workers dug the marl down in the ravine over at Farmer Hopkins' place.

Then one day, around the year 1838, the workers started running into a problem. Every time they dug they found these huge black bones.

"Now here's the funny part," the sculptor said. "Nobody back then had even heard of the word dinosaur. They were living in 1838 and the word dinosaur wasn't even coined (that means invented) until 1841!"

"That's three years," Ian called out.

"Right you are," the sculptor said.

Zoltan groaned and muttered, "Anybody could have figured that out."

Mr. Giannotti explained that the word "dinosaur" was invented by a man named Richard Owen who lived in London, England in 1841. To come up with the name, he studied the bones that were being found in England and decided that they must all come from some family of huge lizards. At that time the only dino bones being found were found in England, not North America.

So Richard Owen took two words from the Greek language Dino and Saurs (SOR-US), which meant "terrible lizard." After a while people took a shortcut by saying dinosaur and that's where the word came from.

"Why did he use a different language for the name?" Zoltan asked. "Why not use English?"

The sculptor chuckled and shrugged his shoulders. "Good question. Maybe back in those times people thought that using a different language to name things would make the thing sound more important and special. It might also show people how smart the person was because he knew another language. Then people would give the person more respect."

"So he was sort of showing off?" Zoltan asked knowingly.

"In a way," he answered. "But then again, if you spent all that time

47

and effort to learn a whole new language you might want to find ways to put that knowledge to work too."

Getting back on the subject he continued: "So they had no idea what these bones really belonged to. They pulled them out of the soil and took them home to use as door stops and window jambs!"

Both boys frowned, not understanding.

"What are those," Ian asked.

"Shhhhhhh!" Zoltan snapped at his brother. "I want to hear this!"

"No, no, good questions are always welcome," Mr. Giannotti said. He explained that a doorstop was anything you use to help hold a door open and a window jamb was anything you use to hold a window open.

Now it was Zoltan's turn to interrupt demanding, "Wait a minute. You mean people had the bones of an actual dinosaur and they used them to hold open the door?"

Ian was off and laughing again. "A dinosaur doorstop? I love it! You should make little Haddys and sell them as doorstops."

"Hmmmmmmm," the sculptor

said. "I think I should have you two visit more often. That's not a bad idea. Maybe after the big fella is done, I'll give that a try."

Mr. Giannotti smiled and then went back to the story.

"Here's the important thing to know, before Haddy, nobody had ever found a whole skeleton, or anything even close that would give scientists an idea of how they looked. Back in those days there had never been more than a bone or two found in any one place."

"So who figured it out?" Zoltan asked.

The sculptor answered, "Nobody, until a man named William Parker

Foulke (FOLK-EE) came to visit here about 20 years after those first bones were found in the marl."

"Farmer Hopkins had a big house and he liked to invite all his friends to come and have dinner there in the summertime," Mr. Giannotti said. "Well one of his friends was Mr. Foulke who happened to be visiting from Pennsylvania and who was a member of the Philadelphia Academy of Natural Sciences in Pennsylvania."

Zoltan was sitting on the edge of his clay seat as the sculptor told the tale.

Ian shouted, "Oh, oh, I know! I can guess! So Foulke saw the dinosaur bones holding the door open and he went crazy and dug up all the bones!"

Mr. Giannotti laughed. "Well, it might have happened that way.

Nobody's really sure. We know he heard the story of giant bones being dug up there and he asked the farmer to allow him and other scientists to come in and start digging again."

Ian opened his mouth to say "wicked" but stopped himself and said, "Whoa!" instead.

The sculptor gave him a wink.

"And?" Zoltan finally burst out. "And then what really happened?"

Chapter Three

"What really happened then is what makes this one of the most famous towns on the planet earth!" Mr. Giannotti said, holding up a copy of a very old newspaper clipping.

The boys read the story that told of how Foulke had those bones dug up and how he showed the bones to a scientist named Joseph Leidy (LID-EE).

Leidy ran the Philadelphia Academy of Natural Sciences. He checked the bones and identified them as belonging to a huge dinosaur that was a lot like an Iguanodon (EE-GWON-OH-DON).

Leidy named the dinosaur Hadrosaurus (Greek for "bulky lizard") foulkii (after the man who discovered it). Foulke's Big Lizard.

The newspaper article showed a picture of a man with dark hair, a beard and moustache sitting beside a giant hadrosaurus bone that was as tall as he was.

The words under the picture read, "Dr. Joseph Leidy, Curator of the

Academy of Natural Sciences, and the bone of the first nearly complete dinosaur skeleton found in North America, Haddonfield, New Jersey, 1858."

"So what made this dinosaur so famous?" Zoltan asked. "Was it the biggest? Or was it the strongest?"

The sculptor frowned. "Bigger and stronger aren't always a claim to fame. No, this dino was famous because it was the first one that was found almost complete. It was the dinosaur that really showed us how huge and amazing these creatures were. It was the one that helped scientists figure out that these guys walked on two legs."

Reading the different newspaper clippings, Zoltan was amazed to learn just how much work went into digging up this dino.

One story told of how, at a depth of about ten feet, they found a jumble of large black bones. These bones made up most of the left side of a skeleton, including part of the hip, nearly all of the front and hind legs, 28 vertebrae and nine teeth.

It went on to say that, "No skull was uncovered."

Zoltan stopped reading and looked up. "No skull? Does that mean it didn't have a head?"

"Aaaaaaaaaah," cried the sculptor. "Now you have stumbled on my big problem with the sculpture! There was no skull. Nobody knows for sure how Haddy's head should look."

Zoltan frowned. "But your wire frame has a head and so do the pictures of hadrosaurs in my science book and in these newspapers. How can that be?"

Chapter Four

"Enter the iguana!" Mr. Giannotti cried holding up a large rubber toy. The boys looked at each other as if they were not very impressed.

"Um, that's a teeny lizard," Ian said pointing to the toy. Then he pointed to the wire frame of the sculpture and said, "That's a giant dinosaur. They don't go together."

Now it was Mr. Giannotti's turn to laugh.

"Absolutely right my friend," he said. "That's what many scientists and artists today have to say about it. But that was all they had as an example back in the 1800s, so that's what they used."

Now the boys were confused. They were picturing in their minds what the giant reptile would look like with an itsy-bitsy iguana head. As serious as he was about dinosaurs, Zoltan cracked up laughing.

"No way!" he said.

"Way. Way," said the sculptor. He went back to the pile of newspaper clippings and shuffled through them for a few moments.

Then he came back with a picture of a huge hadrosaurus skeleton standing in a museum. It had a skull.

When the boys looked from that picture to the one of the iguana they could see how much alike the two shapes were.

"It looks like they just took an iguana skull and magnified it," Zoltan said.

"Precisely!" Mr. Giannotti cried.

"You hit it right on the head."

"Hey, on the head," Ian said. "That's funny."

Zoltan gave his younger brother a warning look and ran his fingers across his own mouth in a motion that meant "zip your lips."

"Let me explain," Mr. Giannotti said. "Foulke and Leidy wanted to put the skeleton on display. It would be the first full dinosaur skeleton in the world."

He continued, "Because Leidy was the curator, the person who was in charge of the Academy of Natural

Sciences, they decided that was the place to set up the skeleton."

"But they didn't have a full skeleton," Ian pointed out. "They only had forty-seven bones. I read that dinosaurs have like two-hundred or more."

The sculptor patted Ian on the shoulder. "Aaaaaaaah, now we're getting to the heart of the matter."

He explained that Foulke figured out a way to make a mold called a cast of the bones and then make copies in plaster, which is like concrete.

"But, like Ian said, they didn't have all of the bones," Zoltan interrupted. "What did they do, make them up?"

There was a long silence as they all realized what he had just said.

"No. No way in the world would scientists make something up," Zoltan said angrily. "That would be crazy!"

"Yeah, that would be crazy," Ian echoed.

Mr. Giannotti smiled. "Well, they were eager to show the world a whole dino and they were so very close. So yes, they fudged it a little."

"A little! A little?" Zoltan was practically shouting. "They put an iguana's head on a hadrosaurus!"

"But who could tell the difference back then," Mr. Giannotti asked reasonably. "They weren't trying to lie to people. They were just making their best guess to fill in the gaps."

Ian nodded in agreement. "After all, they were only human. I mean, they were trying to solve a puzzle."

"They were trying to solve one puzzle by using pieces from a totally different puzzle," Zoltan added.

"That's correct," the sculptor said. "They had help from an English sculptor. Here take a look at this."

Zoltan picked up one of the clippings and read about how sculptor Benjamin Waterhouse Hawkins from England made the first life-sized display of a hadrosaurus skeleton using a copy of the bones made of plaster and the iguana and other dinosaur bones as models for his work.

"This says that the reconstruction of the hadrosaurus is still at the Philadelphia Academy of Natural Sciences," Zoltan told Ian.

He read on about how copies of the copy of the skeleton were made and taken to museums all over the world.

"Whoa, all those copies. All wrong," Ian said. "That's a lot of wrong copies."

"It was a lot of attention for a brand new thing," Mr. Giannotti said.

"If those two scientists and that sculptor hadn't made those guesses and those copies then it would have been many years before people got seriously interested in digging for dinosaur bones."

"As it was," he explained, "the discovery of the Haddonfield Hadrosaurus foulkii sparked the entire dinosaur hunting craze around the world. Expeditions began and soon the T-Rex and others were unearthed."

"Unfortunately, once those big, scary brutes were dug up, poor old, gentle Haddy was completely forgotten," he added. "Few movies feature plant eating dinos and when they do they never mention Haddy or Haddonfield. That's what we hope my statue will change."

"Poor Haddy," said Ian.

"Poor Haddonfield and poor Foulke and Leidy," Zoltan said. "They made a huge discovery and nobody remembers it."

They all looked up at the wire frame of the dinosaur. Ian walked over and patted it, "Don't worry Haddy. We'll get people to remember you."

Then he turned to the sculptor and asked, "But how did they get the bones copied and moved and everything?"

"I guess I should back up and tell you some more of the story," Mr. Giannotti said.

He explained that back when the bones were being dug up by Mr. Foulke there were artists on hand to help give us a picture of how things looked. They made sketches, or quick drawings of how the bones (47 in all including part of the jaw) looked."

"This was because some of the bones were cracked and they wanted to be certain that they at least had a drawing of them while they were here, just in case they broke."

Ian, who loved to draw and wished more than anything to grow up to be a scientist, found this bit of information to be ultra-important. At last he sat still as a statue and listened.

The sculptor went on to tell the boys how each bone was sketched, measured, placed on a board, wrapped in cloth and transported in a straw-filled cart almost a mile to where Foulke was staying in Haddonfield.

The bones were then taken to the museum where the casts were made and the bones were sealed away in special boxes. They are still there today, right in Philadelphia.

"Here Zoltan, take a look at this story," Mr. Giannotti said. "I bet when you go home tonight you two can go on the Internet with your parents and look up a whole lot more information. But this is a good start."

Ian leaned over to look at the old faded photograph of the standing dinosaur skeleton that was made by Hawkins. Then he looked at Mr. Giannotti's wire frame for the statue of Haddy.

"Your head is different," Ian said. "I mean, Haddy's head is different from the one on this statue."

"Good eyes," the sculptor said. Ian adjusted his eyeglasses proudly. Zoltan groaned.

Mr. Giannotti went back to his closet and took out a large rolled up poster. He unrolled it and held it up for them to see. There were several pictures of dinosaurs.

All of them looked a lot like Haddy, but each had a different head. Some had huge things on their heads that stuck up about two feet like a big hat that had been smushed together, tall and flat.

"That one looks like it has a frisbee standing up on its head," Ian said.

"It's called a crest," Mr. Giannotti said.

"You see the first choice was the

iguana and the dinosaur cousin the Iguanodon. But while they are the same size as Haddy, about 30-feet long, they have a beak for a mouth and not a duck-bill."

"Then paleontologists began finding other hadrosaur cousins that had duck bills like the Lambeosaurus, in places like New Mexico and in other countries."

At the mention of New Mexico Zoltan perked up.

Mr. Giannotti explained that the Lambeosaurus, was almost exactly the same as the Hadrosaurus except that it was larger, almost 50-feet long.

"It had this massive two-foot-high crest on top of its head," he said. "But the jaws didn't match and so scientists figured that the heads would be different."

Ian was getting really impatient. He wanted to know how the sculptor had picked this particular head for Haddy.

Mr. Giannotti could see the questions forming in Ian's and Zoltan's minds.

"To pick Haddy's head I did my own research and I even talked to some scientists. In the end, I settled on the head of a Kritosaurus."

Looking at the head of the Kritosaurus they could see that while it didn't have a duck-bill it did seem to fit much better on Haddy's shoulders.

Mr. Giannotti had added the duck-bill and it really looked like it was the best possible choice.

76

Chapter Five

"Sweet," Ian exclaimed.

Mr. Giannotti stared at him. "I beg your pardon?"

"Well, you said I needed a new word," Ian shrugged.

"Right," Mr Giannotti said. "Remind me to give you a dictionary for Christmas."

"Christmas is over already," Ian complained. "How about my birthday? That's in May."

Zoltan was horror-struck by his younger brother's bold talk. The sculptor didn't seem to mind. He thought it was all a very good joke.

"Right," Mr. Giannotti said. "May it is."

Zoltan was ready to explode with aggravation. Here they were, learning about a real live, well dead now, but once live, dinosaur from their town and these two were talking about words.

WORDS! Would he never be free of words?

Poems. Greek words and dictionaries, GRRRRRRR!

Now, instead of thinking about this awesome dinosaur he was back to thinking about his poem for Mrs. Warner. He wanted to rush home and get started looking up facts on the Internet - dinosaur facts, not poem junk.

But he knew his mother would never let him spend all his time on that when the poem of doom was due in just two days.

Now Friday was gone and it was getting too late to even start it.

He really only had the weekend to do it and he was sure he was going to come up empty on ideas. Every time he looked at his journal his mind went as blank as the lined pages in the book.

All this was buzzing in his brain, making him want to scream.

"Is everything O.K.," Mr. Giannotti asked when he saw Zoltan's face turning purple with anger.

Angry tears of frustration prickled up in Zoltan's eyes. He squeezed them shut.

It took a few moments for him to master himself and his temper again. Then he answered.

"I'm just sick of so many words,"

he said. "I have this stupid, stupid, boring poem to write for school and I can't think of any stupid thing to do it on."

Then he added, "Besides, it's winter and poems are always about things like flowers." He stopped himself from saying "and kissing," fearing that Ian would go off again. Too late.

"And kissing!" Ian squealed. "Kissing and flowers! Flowers and kissing." Ian puckered his lips and pretended to kiss the air.

"Oh be quiet!" Zoltan yelled at Ian. "Man, I wish I had to write about science or dinosaurs instead of some dumb poem."

Mr. Giannotti tried very hard not to laugh.

"Hmm, that's serious," he said. "I see your problem. But I think you're mistaken about the whole idea of poetry. In fact, I think you already know a science poem. One about stars."

Mr. Giannotti closed his eyes and looked like he was concentrating very hard. Then he started to recite:

"Twinkle, twinkle little star,
How I wonder what you are!
Up above the world so high,
Like a diamond in the sky.

When the blazing sun is gone,
When she nothing shines upon,

82

Then you show your little light,
Twinkle, twinkle, all the night.

Then the traveler in the dark,
Thanks you for your little spark,
He could not see which way to go,
If you did not twinkle so.

In the dark blue sky you keep,
And so often through my cur-
tains peep,
For you never shut your eye,
Till the sun is in the sky.

'Tis your bright and tiny spark,
Lights the traveler in the dark,
Though I know not what you are,
Twinkle, twinkle, little star."

"That poem is called 'The Star' and it was written by two sisters in the year 1806," he said as the boys looked very impressed. "The sisters were Ann and Jane Taylor who lived in Colchester, England."

Zoltan didn't know what to say. He had only heard the first few lines of that poem when he was very little. He always thought it was just a baby song. Now he realized that there was much more to it than that.

"How about a poem about Haddy," Mr. Giannotti asked. "There was a dino named Haddy, who was a good guy and not baddy."

Zoltan looked as if he had been hit by the biggest idea of his life.

"I can do that," he said. "I can write a poem about a hadrosaurus. That used to hold the door open for us!"

"Hey that rhymes," Ian said.

"DUH!" Zoltan answered.

"Sweet," Mr. Giannotti shouted.

Both boys looked shocked.

Then Ian started to laugh. Mr. Giannotti started to laugh, too. Zoltan was so relieved that he could think of something interesting to use for his poem, he started to laugh too.

"It's pretty late in the day, you'd better get going home," Mr. Giannotti said. "If you hurry, you may still have time to have your mom or dad help you look up a few facts on the Internet before bedtime."

"Can I help?" Ian asked Zoltan. "Please? Please-oh-pleasy-weezy?"

Zoltan looked his brother up and down. Ian drove him crazy, but he was really good to have around sometimes. Ian was also really good at rhymes. Still, that didn't stop Zoltan from deciding to torture him, just a little.

"Well, maybe," he said.

"YEAH!" Ian cried, hopping up and down.

"BUT!" Zoltan called above the noise. "You would have to be really quiet and not hover over me the whole time."

"Absolutely," Ian said. "No hovering. No siree. Um, uh, what's hovering again?"

Ian asked this while he was so close to his older brother he was practically standing on Zoltan's feet. He was also bouncing up and down on his toes.

"What you are doing right now!" Zoltan said.

Ian backed up. "Got it!" he cried.

Chapter Six

After moving the clay, all the talk and excitement, plus a quick run down the snowy lane back to their house, the boys were starving.

They burst through the door calling, "Mom! Mom!"

They could smell dinner cooking and heard their littlest brother Avery, who was just four years old, making noise in the kitchen.

Ian was the first one to find their mother in the kitchen. She was making hot cocoa.

"You two took so long I thought you decided to move to New Mexico without me," she said.

The smell of the delicious, sweet hot chocolate made them realize how hungry they were after their long talk.

"Mom, there was a Haddy-saurus right here in town and Mr. Giannotti is making it into a statue," Ian blurted out.

Zoltan groaned and moved into the space between Ian and his mother.

"No, no, no," he said impatiently. "Not Haddy-saurus! H-A-D-R-O-S-A-U-R-U-S. And he's not making it into a statue. He's making a statue of it. Geez!"

"Whatever," Ian said. He was annoyed at being corrected again by his big brother. "It's so wicked!"

Zoltan was determined to keep their mom's attention so he ignored his brother and continued.

"So, mom," he said. "You knew that dinosaurs used to be right here in Haddonfield and you never told us? That's mean."

Mom poured the cocoa into mugs and dropped fat white marshmallows on top. She carried the mugs to the table and sat down with a mug of her own.

"Me, me, me," Avery shouted, racing across the room to grab a marshmallow. Mom gave him a little mug with one fluffy white puffball floating on top.

The boys rushed over and began to spoon up the yummy hot liquid. Between slurps and saying "mmmmmmm" Zoltan eyed his mother. He was wondering if she would answer him.

Finally she did.

"I am a little embarrassed to say this, but I didn't know until just a few days ago," she said. "Your father didn't know either. We just read it in the newspaper when the Garden Club decided to mark the 145th anniversary by asking Mr. Giannotti to make the statue."

Mom explained that she planned to tell the boys about the dinosaur, but wanted to wait until the statue was a little farther along. She had talked to Mr. Giannotti that morning as he was carrying supplies into his studio.

He told her that the boys could come by any time to help him or to watch him work.

"So, what did you learn from Mr. Giannotti," she asked as she got up and began to put dinner on the table.

As the boys all dug in to their chicken and french fries they took turns telling the story of the Haddonfield Hadrosaurs.

Of course, Ian wanted to tell the funny part first. He told Mom about how the massive bones had been used as doorstops because nobody knew what they were.

"A dinosaur as a doorstop," he giggled. "I just love that part!"

While Zoltan really liked that

part too, he chose to tell the more serious, scientific and historical details.

He tried very hard to remember all the names, but it was hard.

"There was this guy named William Foulke who went to dinner at farmer Hopkins' house and he heard about the dinosaur bones," Zoltan recounted. "Then he called this other scientist from Philadelphia. I can't remember his name."

"Leidy," Ian added. Zoltan glared at him. He hated it when his younger brother tried to make him look stupid.

Ian shrugged his shoulders. "I only remembered it because it rhymes with giddy. I was laughing a lot and so Leidy, giddy. Get it?"

Rhymes again! Zoltan started to get frustrated again.

"Whatever," Zoltan said." Anyway, Leidy and Foulke dug up the bones and they took them to the museum in Philadelphia…"

Ian interrupted, "Can we go see them? Please? Oh pleasy-weezy?"

Mom laughed. "Yes, we can all go this Saturday," she said. "Your father loves dinosaurs."

Just then they heard their father's pick-up truck pull up to the house.

"Good timing," Ian said.

"He always comes home at this time," Zoltan said. He could not believe there were so many interruptions tonight.

"Hi, Dad," Zoltan called.

"Hi, Dad," Ian called.

Avery, who didn't want to eat his dinner and wanted to go play shouted, "I hate dinner, Dad."

"Hello to you, too," their father said as he took turns hugging and kissing everybody around the table.

Their father sniffed the air. "Hot cocoa, chicken and fries," he announced. "Wicked!"

Ian laughed.

"We saw a dinosaur today," Ian announced.

"Iiiiiiiaaannnnnnn," Zoltan said in a warning way. "We did not see a real dinosaur. We saw a wire frame that will become a statue of a dinosaur."

Their father took his place at the table and looked at the boys. He guessed they'd been to visit the sculptor down the street.

"How is Mr. Giannotti," he asked.

"Great," Ian answered.

"And how is Haddy coming along," he asked. "I think we should definitely make a trip to the Philadelphia Academy of Natural Sciences to see the bones and the sculpture there."

Mom explained that they were just talking about that. She told him about their idea of going on Saturday. Dad agreed right away. He was always ready to go on a road trip.

"So what did you learn," he asked the boys.

Finally Zoltan got a chance to talk about the dinosaurs.

He re-told the story of Foulke and Leidy. Then he told his father all about how careful everyone had to be with the bones.

He told about how there were 47 bones found, almost a whole skeleton. He also was sure to explain that it was the first time scientists could really understand what a dinosaur looked like and how it must have walked on two feet.

Ian interrupted to tell about the dino doorstops and how Leidy rhymes with giddy.

"And they never found the skull," Zoltan added triumphantly. "So Mr. Giannotti had to do all this research to figure out what kind of head to put on

Haddy's shoulders. He picked a Kritosaurus."

This was all new to their parents. They hadn't been at the sculptor's studio to see all the pictures, books and newspaper clippings. It was hard for them to picture in their minds how the different dinosaurs looked.

When dinner and dessert were finished, their father stopped them from heading for the television set.

"Homework all done?" he asked them.

"Yes," said Ian.

"Almost," said Zoltan. "I have a poem due in two days."

His father looked at him sympathetically. When he was in school, he too, had hated writing stories and essays - especially poems. Like Zoltan, he liked to play chess and play music.

"Well, you have to do what your teacher assigns," he said. "What does the poem have to be about?"

"It can be about anything," Zoltan said. "I was thinking about doing one on the hadrosaurus."

Zoltan waited and held his breath. Would his dad think this was a dumb idea? Would he force him to write one about something boring?

He didn't have to worry. His father grinned at him and gave him a squeeze. "That's the best poem idea I have ever heard," he said. "That's great."

Phew!

Zoltan told about the star poem Mr. Giannotti recited.

"I never knew there was so much to that poem," Ian added. "I mean, wow. That was so interesting. It really made me see stars in a different way."

"Well let's see if we can see Haddonfield and this dinosaur in a different way," their father said.

He sat at the computer and turned it on. The screen glowed blue and then up popped the gray screen with all the little icons, those little pictures that tell you which program is which.

There was one with a big letter W that stood for "word processor." That was the typing program Mom used to write letters and do her work.

Zoltan had been allowed to use it to write his last book report on Benjamin Franklin. It was great. He got to type instead of writing everything out longhand.

It made him feel very important and grown-up to be using that program.

On the screen, there was a little picture of a camera. Their father had a special camera that stored the pictures, in the computer instead of on film.

When you plugged the camera into the computer and clicked on the picture on the screen the pictures from the camera showed up on the screen. Then you could print them out on the printer.

There was even one icon that was a bunch of wild looking colored balls.

That was where all the games were stored in the computer. Zoltan loved playing the different adventure games.

But this time they were going to click the arrow on the big letter e that stood for Explorer - the Internet Explorer. In Zoltan's mind even the name was awesome.

Because the Internet linked a computer in one house to millions of other computers around the world in places like libraries, newspapers and magazines, it was a great place to learn new things.

There were also websites. These were places your computer could visit that were created by teachers, scientists and just plain people, in order to share information.

Each website had pages and pages of pictures and stories, and information you could read and print out on your own printer at home.

Zoltan had seen his father print-out pictures of sailboats and maps for places they wanted to go hiking and kayaking. He had seen his mother print out directions for how to get to new places and recipes for new desserts.

Zoltan and Ian were allowed to play some games on the Internet, but they had never used it as a tool to look up information. The house rule was that kids were only allowed to use the Internet when a grownup was helping.

Now with Dad sitting at the keyboard and typing away things were pretty exciting.

"O.K.," he said to the boys as he clicked on the e. "I am going to use something called a search engine. That is a website that helps you search for information very fast."

On the screen a long thin box appeared. It looked like one blank line from Zoltan's journal book.

A blinking black line appeared at the beginning of the box. Their father typed and words appeared in the box.

It read: New Jersey Dinosaur.

Their father pressed the key marked ENTER. Immediately the screen filled with dozens of lines of typing.

They could see the words HADROSAURUS foulkii and Haddonfield repeated over and over again. Their father explained that if the words were written in blue then they could click on those words and go to the page on that subject.

The first page they clicked on took them to a website created by the Garden Club. There on the screen was a picture of Mr. Giannotti and the wire frame of Haddy!

"Whoa," Ian gasped. "It looks just like what we just saw. That's amazing."

For the next hour they took turns sitting in the chair in front of the computer and going through the pages. They even printed out some of the most interesting ones from museums.

On one page they were surprised to learn that the only reason New Jersey isn't as well known for having dinosaurs buried there is that scientists were not able to explore there.

In New Jersey, most of the land is what they call developed. That means the land is owned by people who built houses and buildings on top of the land.

They learned that places like New Mexico have more open space that is owned as parks. Because nothing was built there the wind, rain and time have been free to wear away the soil. When the dirt was worn down, bones were exposed.

Then scientists would find them and start digging. The rest is history.

Reading all this, Zoltan got really excited.

"Dad, I think this means that there could be lots of dinosaur bones all over New Jersey and we could still find them," he said. "They never found Haddy's skull. That means I could find it."

"Or I could find it," Ian said.

"Or maybe somebody already found it in 1838 and is using it as a coffee table," Zoltan added.

"You remembered the year the bones were first discovered," Dad said. "I am very impressed!"

Zoltan grinned, "Well, not exactly. It's still there on the computer screen behind you."

Ian giggled.

Their dad groaned.

"Alright. You out smarted me," he said. "But it's time to go to bed. You can both dream of digging up dinosaurs in the yard."

Chapter Seven

He was rocking and rocking. There was the sound of birds calling SKREE-SKREE. Then he heard a swish. SPLASH!

It was a loud splashing sound, like the world's biggest paddle was hitting the water. It was hot and sunny and Zoltan was sitting in the red kayak. It looked like he was in the ocean!

For some strange reason he wasn't scared. This was really amazing. The water stretched for miles in one direction it looked as if the water went on forever.

Then the water nearby erupted like a volcano. But instead of lava, up splashed the head of a hadrosaurus!

Zoltan stared at it. "Wow!" he said.

"Wow," answered the duck-billed giant. This one didn't have a crest or a beak or look like an inflated iguana. It looked exactly like Mr. Giannotti's Haddy.

Zoltan gasped in surprise. "You can talk!" he said.

"You can talk," the beast replied.

"I must be dreaming," Zoltan said.

"That's a safe bet," replied the dinosaur.

But Zoltan didn't wake up. He had too many questions to ask before he let that happen.

"What are you doing in the ocean," he asked. "I thought you lived in the mud?"

"Remember that New Jersey was under 100 feet of seawater during my time and the beach was in Philadelphia," Haddy replied.

Zoltan squinted in the hot sun. "Yes, but you don't have flippers. You're not really a sea swimmer are you?"

The dinosaur chuckled. "True. But I didn't talk either. This is just a dream and a really interesting way to help you remember what it was like when I did exist," Haddy replied.

"Cool," Zoltan said. He blinked at the sun and in the blink of an eye he found himself much closer to the beach. By paddling for just a short time he was able to pull the kayak right up onto the shore and step out onto the sand.

"How's that," Haddy asked as he stepped out of the water and towered 30-feet over Zoltan. The great beast lumbered over to a nearby bush and began to chomp away at the leaves. The dinosaur walked on its thick hind legs, swishing its long thick tail.

Seeing that tail reminded Zoltan of the rudder on his father's sailboat. Rudders are used to steer in the water and he could now imagine Haddy steering himself along the shore to cool off and maybe find some water plants to root up and eat.

Haddy used his front legs, which had hooves like a horse, to paw at the branches.

"Being at the beach always makes me so hungry," Haddy said as he made a meal of the bush.

"You shouldn't talk with your mouth full," Zoltan said.

"Sorry," Haddy mumbled as he swallowed. Then he yawned and Zoltan could see that while the front of his mouth looked like a huge duck bill there were teeth inside Haddy's cheeks.

"What are those," he asked pointing to the teeth. "I didn't know you had teeth."

"They're cheek teeth and they help me crunch the sticks," the beast answered.

Zoltan sat down on the sand and watched the waves roll in to the shore. He wondered how in the world the dinosaur's bones could have made it all the way from here, across the water to Haddonfield.

He looked at the horizon and tried to imagine how far away Haddonfield was from Philadelphia, about a half an hour by car. About 25 miles?

He heard Haddy crunching behind him and saw some of the leaves from the bush fly past on a breeze that carried them onto the water.

The leaves floated. Then they were carried out on the outgoing tide. The current pulled them out to sea and they quickly disappeared from view.

Zoltan's eyes widened with surprise. Of course! That must be the answer.

"Haddy, when your bones were found you were headless," Zoltan said.

There was an enormous choking sound from behind him. A sputtering and then, "WHAT? Me, headless?"

Even though he was sure this was a dream, Zoltan didn't want to hurt the animal's feelings. "Um, sorry. But you know about the cycle of life right? Born, live, die. Everybody does it sometime."

The hadrosaurus looked insulted.

"Sorry."

Haddy shook it's head and said, "I suppose so. I just don't like to think about it. So what were you saying?"

"I was thinking that if you, or any creature, died here on the beach you might fall in the water or you might already be in the water and die of drowning," he added.

"Such lovely thoughts," the dinosaur said sarcastically. "You should write poetry."

Zoltan eyed the beast sharply. Poetry again. He just could not get away from it, even in his dreams.

"Thanks a lot," Zoltan said. "Let's not turn this into a nightmare by talking about that subject."

Now Haddy said, "Sorry."

"So if some creature died they might be taken out to sea by the tide and then sink into the bottom of the sea bed," Zoltan said. "Maybe the head got ripped off by a shark and floated away.

Maybe it got disconnected some other way and the tide brought it back to shore in what is now Philadelphia."

"That's using your head," the dinosaur said. "Or were you using my head? In any case, it makes a lot of sense."

Zoltan was feeling very sleepy now. He closed his eyes and lay back on the warm beach.

Chapter Eight

He felt a poking feeling in his side. He must have rolled over onto Haddy's tail, he thought as he rolled over.

Poke, poke, poke. There it was again. He opened his eyes to see what the problem was and saw his littlest brother, Avery. He was poking him with a toy dinosaur.

"Get up," he said. "Get up now.

It's sad day. We go to see dinosaurs at the newzeeum."

Huh? A sad day? Newzeeum?

"Oh, no, no, no. You mean it's Saturday and we're going to the museum," Zoltan corrected as he sat up in bed.

It had been a dream. He knew it, but was still sorry to have to wake up.

Avery stamped his foot and poked his oldest brother with the toy T-rex again. "C'mon!"

After dressing and tooth brushing and all of the morning things, he went downstairs where he found everyone rushing around.

Dad was pouring coffee. Ian was crunching a granola bar and reading the funnies from the newspaper. Mom was filling a thermos with coffee and packing up juice boxes and snacks for the trip to Philadelphia.

Ian looked up from what he was reading and sputtered, "Zomuff!"

"You shouldn't talk with your mouth full," their mother said to Ian.

Ian swallowed and repeated, "Zoltan!"

"Somebody slept late," Dad said as he sipped his coffee and looked at a map of the road that would take them to the Academy of Natural Sciences and the dinosaur museum inside.

They would have to travel on the highway to the Benjamin Franklin Bridge and into Pennsylvania. The bridge would take them straight into the city where the museum was located. Since they had never been to the museum before Dad had to check the map to figure out the best route, or way to go.

"I was having this dream," Zoltan said. "I dreamed I was kayaking in the ocean with a Hadrosaur and we went to the beach in Philadelphia."

"That must have been some dream," Mom said. "You can tell us all about it while we drive. Everybody saddle up! Into the van."

They all piled into the family's big tan-colored mini van and buckled up their seatbelts. As they drove along Zoltan began to tell about his dream.

Mom looked at the map, while their dad drove. They all listened to Zoltan describe what everything looked like when he was in his dream kayaking with Haddy.

When Zoltan paused for breath, Mom said, "This is starting to sound like a pretty strange dream."

Dad interrupted, "Well it really wasn't that strange a dream. After all,

all these towns we are driving past, and everything right up to Philly, was once under a hundred feet of seawater. So that was one smart dream."

Zoltan grinned. He loved it when his dad thought he was smart. He thought his father was the smartest person he knew.

Then he told all about his idea that the head of the hadrosaurus had floated there and sunk like a ship wreck.

When he was finished telling it he held his breath. He was hoping his father would not think this was really silly.

"Now that's very interesting," his

father said. "That was a good use of logic. You used your knowledge of the dinosaur and put it together with what you know about kayaking and the ocean tides. Good work!"

Zoltan felt his face get warm. That was better than he had hoped.

"So maybe the head floated to Grandma's house up north," Ian said.

"Maybe it got washed in with the tide back to Philadelphia and got buried in the sand there," said Mom. "Hey, we're over the bridge everybody! Next stop, the museum."

They drove into town and started turning this way and that through the maze of city streets.

Dad spoke up. "Maybe it never washed away at all and someone in 1838 dug it up right here and their great, great, great grandchildren are using it as a coffee table," he said.

Ian gasped. "Hey! That's just what Zoltan said to Mr. Giannotti yesterday. Remember Zoltan?"

"Great minds think alike," Mom said.

"Great minds think for themselves," Dad added.

"Great minds don't miss the turn to the museum!" Zoltan cried as their father missed the turn at the museum sign.

"Grrrrrrrrr," said Dad. "We'll go around the block. That's what happens when your head is filled with hadrosaurus."

Chapter Nine

At last they arrived at the Academy of Natural Sciences and headed into the museum.

As they entered, they were given a map of the museum. It showed all the different things they could see, which in a museum are called exhibits.

The map showed Dinosaur Hall, The Paleo Lab, The Mesozoic Mural,

The Time Machine, The Big Dig and much more.

"What's a Paleo Lab?" Ian asked.

"That's short for Paleolithic," their dad explained. "The Paleolithic Era is the beginning of when humans lived on the planet approximately 31,000 years ago."

"How do we know that?" Zoltan asked. His faith in paleontology had been shaken a bit when he learned that they had "fudged" Haddy's reconstruction.

"Because they found some paintings on cave walls in France," Mom answered. "In the cave of Chauvet Pont-D-Arc."

Everyone looked at Mom. "It's written right here on the museum map," she said with a grin.

"Well, I know about people," Ian said. "Let's go see Dinosaur Hall."

"Dino Ball! Dino Ball," Avery chanted. He hopped up and down. Everyone laughed.

They all headed to the Dinosaur Hall. Zoltan was in the lead. Ian was behind him and Avery was behind them with their parents.

Suddenly, Zoltan stopped and Ian nearly tumbled head-first over his older brother.

"Hey!" he cried. Ian glared up at Zoltan and saw that he was pointing straight up. Following the direction of his brother's hand he looked way up and saw a massive dinosaur skeleton standing right in front of them. It had teeth that were longer than Ian's hand.

"Is that Haddy?" Ian asked.

"That can't possibly be a hadrosaurus," Zoltan said. "It has teeth and it's way too big. No duck-bill."

They heard their father reading something out loud from behind them. "The museum features a fully constructed Gigantasaurus, the largest meat-eater ever to walk the earth!"

They looked the monster up and down. It towered over them.

Zoltan walked over to the sign his father was reading and read to himself. It said that the Gigantasaurus was the longest meat-eating dinosaur yet discovered. It was between 44 and 46 feet (13.5-14.3 meters) and weighed about eight tons. It stood 12 feet tall (at the hips).

Zoltan could not help laughing at what he read next. He decided to read it out loud, "It walked on two legs and had a brain the size of a banana."

Ian cracked up. Even his parents laughed. Avery shouted, "I want a banana!"

It was hard to read these signs out loud because the words were new and most were long and tricky. Still, he managed to sound out the words as he went.

He continued to read aloud, "It had enormous jaws with eight-inch long serrated teeth."

"What's serrated," Ian asked.

"It means like a saw," Dad answered.

Zoltan started again, "...serrated teeth in a six-foot (1.8 m) long skull. Gigantasaurus was from the mid-cretaceous period. It lived about 100 million years ago."

"Hey, mid-cretaceous is about when Haddy lived," Ian added.

"Where is Haddy?" Zoltan asked. He looked around the hall but could not see anything that looked like the hadrosaurus.

Then their Dad pointed and said, "I think that may be it over there."

Sure enough, there was Haddy with its iguana skull and all standing tall in the museum.

It was an awesome feeling to look up and see those bones. It made the whole story of the hadrosaurs more real. Now Zoltan understood why Foulke, Leidy and the sculptor, Hawkins, decided to "fudge it."

He realized that at that time this room must have been empty. The Haddonfield Hadrosaurus foulkii discovery must have been the only giant lizard in the room. People must have been very impressed.

He thought, "When it came to making these bones stand up here, something was way, way, better than nothing." He also realized it would not have been nearly as interesting or impressive without a head and with bones missing.

Really, they had done an amazing job. If you didn't know the head was supposed to be different it was a really impressive beast.

"What do you think," his father asked. "Did they do a good thing or a bad thing by making it this way?"

"Good," he answered. "Definitely good."

Now, as they walked through the museum Zoltan tried hard to imagine what it must have been like for a nine-year-old or even a grown-up to walk there with only the hadrosaurus as the star of the show.

O.K., maybe there were one or two other bones and fossils, old shark teeth and stuff, but Haddy must have been a superstar back in those days. Foulke and Leidy must have been more famous than the President.

They spent most of the morning just wandering around and looking at the different skeletons.

They wandered from floor to floor seeing different exhibits of bones, teeth, horns and fossils.

At one point Ian pulled Zoltan over to a large glass case and showed him that another famous scientist had lived in Haddonfield.

Edward Drinker Cope lived in Haddonfield in 1868, ten years after Haddy was taken to the museum. He was one of the very first paleontologists and he was even in charge of running the Academy after Leidy left.

"Mom look at this," Ian said. "This says that Cope started as a scientist when he was just eight years old! That's how old I am!"

It was true. When Cope was just eight years old his parents had taken him to visit the museum at the Academy of Natural Sciences and there, he fell in love with the idea of hunting for ancient bones, teeth and horns.

Ian was leaping up and down with excitement. "Look, Dad," he said. "It says that Cope loved to draw and when he was my age and visited here he made drawings of what he saw and some of those drawings are kept here today!"

Before he even asked, his mother reached into the large canvas bag she was carrying over her shoulder and took out Ian's drawing pad and a pencil. His eyes lit up.

"Thanks!" he scurried away, like a squirrel with a nut, to go and sketch pictures of the skeletons.

Zoltan continued to read about Cope. He learned that the house he once lived in had been bought by the town in 1924 and destroyed to make way for the new Town Hall.

"That stinks," Zoltan said to his father.

His father nodded in agreement, but added, "People don't always appreciate things or people when they come from their own little town."

"Until you learned that the hadrosaurus was found in Haddonfield you thought it was a pretty boring place," he said. "Before people learned how important and interesting paleontology was, they didn't think much of people like Mr. Cope."

Zoltan looked surprised, "You mean they probably just thought he was a silly man who liked to play in the muck and dig big holes in the town?"

"Something like that," Dad answered.

Avery was beginning to cry because he was tired of hiking around the museum and everyone was getting hungry. Everyone except Ian who would have been happy to live in front of the displays with his drawing pad for the rest of the year.

"Time to get rolling," Mom said. Dad agreed and they made their way out of the museum, waving goodbye to the copy of Haddy's skeleton as they left.

In the car, on the way home, everyone was silent, except Avery. He was singing, "Dinosaw, dinosaw I saw a dinosaw!"

"Dino-saur!" both older brothers corrected.

Chapter Ten

Saturday was almost over. The trip to Philadelphia had been amazing. Zoltan's head felt like it weighed two more pounds because of all the new facts stuffed inside.

But now it was time to get down to business. It was Saturday night. Dinner was over. Ian and Avery were watching television and he knew it was time to tackle the Poem of Doom.

Sitting at the dining room table Zoltan stared down at the blank pages of his journal and frowned. How hard could it be? It was just rhymes and facts mixed together, right?

He tried to remember some of the rhymes he was thinking at Mr. Giannotti's studio. He began to write.

"Haddonfield had a hadrosaurus."

He stopped and looked at the rhyme. Not bad. Maybe if he just told the story of Haddy and tried to make it rhyme as much as possible it would work.

Just then his father came in and sat down at the table with him.

"What are you up to?" he asked. "I thought there was never any home-work on weekends."

"Not usually," he answered. "But remember I told you I have this poem project to do?"

His father slapped his hand to his forehead. "Right! The 'Poem of Doom.' So what's it going to be about?"

In answer he picked up the words he'd just written and held the page up for his father to read. He was very relieved when his father smiled.

"Good idea," he said. "Need some help?"

Zoltan explained that he was going to try and write the poem like telling a story only with rhymes.

"In that case, how about if you take a piece of scrap paper and make a list of all the facts you want to use in order. Then you can write rhyming words next to them," his father suggested.

He demonstrated by taking a piece of loose-leaf paper from a pile on the table. He used a ruler to make a line down the center of the page.

On the left side of the line he wrote Haddonfield and on the right he wrote had and hadrosaurus. Then on the left he wrote Leidy and on the right side he wrote city, giddy. He underlined the letters that made the rhymes.

Zoltan liked this system. It made poetry more scientific to him and easier to see. For the first time his father smiled and started out of the room. "Just holler if you need me."

For more than an hour, Zoltan made his list. He decided that tonight would be list night. Tomorrow he would put it all together as a poem.

This turned out to be a very good plan. He finished his list with plenty of time to watch cartoons with his brothers.

When his father asked if he was all done he explained that this was the first time, since Mrs. Warner had given the assignment, he felt relaxed. He knew he could do this. In fact, he was feeling kind of excited about it now.

"Great," he said. "Thanks Dad."

Chapter Eleven

After waking to a big breakfast of eggs and sausages, then playing in the snow and sledding, Zoltan finally sat down in the late afternoon to complete his poem.

He went over his list of facts and rhyming words. Zoltan moved the words around and around on the page. He was making a puzzle fit together and enjoying every minute of it.

He wrote until dinner and then took a break. After dinner he was right back at it. He hardly noticed when Ian and Avery went in to watch television or play on the computer. He ate his dessert at the table while he worked and only stopped now and again to yell, "Will somebody please lower the TV? I'm working here!"

Finally, Ian came snooping around to see what his older brother was doing.

"How's the 'Poem of Doom' coming?" he asked. He expected to see his older brother pouting and angry. He was very surprised to see him smiling in triumph.

At last Zoltan had his poem finished. Words, science, something other than kissing and flowers had gone into making it.

"Done," Zoltan said.

"Done?" Ian asked.

"Done?" his mother asked as she, too, came into the room. His father heard the commotion and came in too.

"Well, how did we do," his father asked.

"Great!" Zoltan answered. "Here it is."

He handed his father the finished copy of the poem in his journal. "Read it out loud," Ian insisted.

"If your brother says so, I will," his father said.

"Yes, but you read it," Zoltan said. "I hate being the center of attention. I get too nervous."

Our Doorstop Dinosaur

By Zoltan Magyar
Mrs. Warner's Class - GRADE 3

Haddonfield had a Hadrosaurus,
right here in our town.
He wasn't really scary, like those others of renown.

During a time they called Cretaceous,
New Jersey wasn't so built up.
It was quite spacious.

Haddy was a gentle creature,
not the kind that movies feature.

Being herbivorous he surely didn't
make anyone nervous.

He snacked on plants,
and never had rants,
or tirades like a T-Rex.
No scary muscles would he flex.

Old Haddy lived life nice and quiet,
with no other dinos in his diet.

When he died his bones sank into the marl
- a kind of crumbly soil used in the gar-
den by my Great-Great-Uncle Carl.

For many years people came here to
buy the marl,
until the workers in the pit hit a snarl.

All those bones were in the way,
they dug them up night and day.

Nobody knew the big old bones came
from a Hadrosaurus.
They used the ones they found
to prop doors open for us!

One day a man named William Foulke
came to our little town.
A scientist from Philadelphia,
he traveled all around.

He heard the stories of big bones
pulled from the marl.

Turns out Mr. Foulke knew lots more than
Great-Great-Uncle Carl.

He said those bones came from a time, long, long before.
Then the scientist turned and saw Haddy's bone stopping the door.

"Gadzooks!" he gasped. "That is no dog bone you have there.
It's from a dinosaur. It's very old and needs special care!"

The people thought the scientist must have slipped a gear.
"A dino-what?
You aren't being clear!"

"A giant lizard," Foulke tried to explain,
but in 1857 nobody knew them by that name.

But Foulke knew a man, named Joseph Leidy,
who would come from a big city
to make this discovery.

The two would soon be famous,
and travel from sea to sea.
All because of that dinosaur,
that lived so close to me.

So Foulke showed them all,
by digging up the Hadrosaurus.
By 1858 he had almost every bone spread out before us.

Well, most of them anyway.
Something's missing to this day.

There was no skull.

No head to put on Haddy's shoulders.
It may still be down there
deep underneath the boulders.

To satisfy our curiosity,
artists have tried different kinds of
heads, to give us something we could
see.

So in the Academy of Natural Sciences
in Philadelphia, Haddy has the head of
an iguana.
You can go see it if you wanna.

In Haddonfield a sculptor named John
Giannotti made a huge Haddy
whose head came from a Kritosaurus.
That certainly won't bore us.

I like them all.
Each Haddy head they make.

Still, I have this feeling I can't shake.
I want to be the one who manages to
find it.

Like Great-Great-Uncle Carl,
I'm in the marl
each chance I get.

I even made a bet
That I would be the one to
Dig up old Haddy's noggin.

I don't mind the muck,
If I have luck
while I'm sloggin'.

You never know. The going's slow.

Still, every day I dig.

I figure you can't miss it.
It must be really big!

When his father finished reading everyone clapped and clapped. Ian jumped around trying to recite parts of it.

"Leidy from the city," he repeated. "I like that even more than Leidy was giddy. Cool!"

"That was amazing," his mom said and hugged him so tight he could hardly breathe.

"That was incredible," his father added. "I wish I could have done poems like that when I was in third grade."

Zoltan was very pleased. "It was really the system you made with the lists that made it easy. Is it too long? Shouldn't poems be short?"

"It's perfect," his father said. "It's like the old epic poems. That's a poem that tells a story, usually a true story. Those can fill whole books."

This was excellent news. He hadn't just written a poem. He had written an epic poem. That sounded very important.

He could not believe it. He could hardly wait to get to school tomorrow, see Mrs. Warner and hand in his work.

Chapter Twelve

When the school bus returned to West End Avenue it must have looked as if a blue and yellow lightning bolt flew off. Zoltan, in his blue and yellow coat, streaked across the lawn and into the house.

He dropped his backpack on the porch and banged the door shut behind him. In his hand was his journal, he was waving it as he shouted, "MOM!

Mom! I got an A-plus! I got an A-plus!"

His mother came rushing into the room just as Ian stomped in behind his older brother and banged the door shut.

"You could have waited for me," he complained as he stomped the snow off his boots onto the rug. Pouting, he flopped down onto the big easy chair in the corner.

Zoltan ignored him and thrust the book at his mother. "Look!"

His mother opened the book and flipped through the pages until she stopped at a big sticker with a smiling dinosaur on it. Next to the sticker was a big red letter A and a plus sign.

The teacher had also written a note that said, "You really got the hang of the epic poem. Great work. We will read this in science class on Wednesday!"

This had been a great day. He could not believe how happy writing this poem had made him.

"Can I go show it to Mr. Giannotti," Zoltan asked.

Mom thought this was a very good idea. She gave Zoltan and Ian permission to visit their neighbor.

"Be back before dark," she warned. "It's Monday and I'm sure you both have homework to do."

After kissing Mom good-bye they boys rushed out the door. Zoltan held his journal tight in his hand and ran all the way to the sculptor's studio.

When they arrived they knocked on the door and Mr. Giannotti opened it. He was splattered with clay from head to foot and looked very tired but very happy.

"Hey!" the sculptor cried. "My two favorite helpers. Come on in. I've been hoping you two would be back to see my progress."

They entered the studio. It had a wonderful smell like wet soil on a summer day. It was the smell of clay; lots and lots of clay.

They looked at the spot where the wire frame had stood. Now they saw it was almost entirely covered in clay.

"Whoa," Ian gasped.

"Pretty sweet, huh?," Mr. Giannotti said. "I have hardly slept a wink since you were here last. I just started and couldn't seem to stop."

While they could see he still had a long way to go before he was finished, it was really starting to take shape. Haddy was coming back to life.

It was very exciting to see the progress. Looking at the statue, Zoltan felt as if he were meeting an old friend.

He walked around it, patted the clay gently and whispered, "Hi Haddy. Good to see you again."

"What do you think," Mr. Giannotti said. "Real enough?"

"I think it looks just like him," Zoltan said.

The sculptor was a little puzzled by this, but he figured it was a compliment.

"So what else is new in the world," he asked the boys. "I have just been here in my own little world of clay."

Now Zoltan remembered why he'd come. "I wrote the poem I was telling you about. Here. Wanna see?"

The sculptor wiped his hands on a clean towel and then carefully took the journal book. He didn't want to get it all muddy.

"Wowie zowie!" he cried. "Look at that grade. And a dino sticker too?"

He sat down on a wooden bench that was splattered with clay and read the poem. He must have read it twice because it was a long time before he spoke.

"I love it," he announced. "I was wondering, could I have a copy of this to show the Garden Club people? I would really like it if you could read this when the statue is unveiled on Lantern Lane in the Fall."

Zoltan was in shock. He loved the idea of having his poem read when Haddy was placed in the center of town. But he would rather not be the guy to read it and have everyone staring at him.

He shuffled his feet and looked at the statue that was taking shape.

The sculptor saw him hesitate. "If you'd rather not, I will understand."

"I guess it would be O.K. But I'd rather you read it than me," he said.

The sculptor smiled. "Well, Fall is months away," he said. "Maybe you'll change your mind by then."

It was getting late and the boys said good-bye. Zoltan promised to ask his father to make a copy of the poem on the machine in his office.

They happily trudged home as the sun was setting. After doing their homework they helped Mom set the table.

Just when they thought they couldn't wait one more minute to eat their father came in calling, "Food for a starving man! What's for dinner?"

Zoltan rushed up to his father and handed him his journal book.

"I'm hungry," his father laughed. "But not hungry enough to eat a book!"

"Ha, ha," Zoltan said. "It's my poem."

His father took the book and headed into the dining room. "First things first, he said and winked at Ian. Then he kissed their mother and said hello.

Zoltan was getting frustrated. He could hardly wait.

At last, Dad sat down at the table and opened the journal. Like Mom, he flipped to the page with the sticker and grinned.

Zoltan could not stop himself from pointing to the page and saying, "Look, she wrote epic poem. Just like you said!"

He also told his father about Mr. Giannotti's request for a copy of the poem and about reading it at Town Center in the Fall.

Once again, his father understood how he felt about being up in front of everybody.

"I know that's not really your favorite thing," he said.

"I hate it," Zoltan said.

"You hated having to write a poem and look how that turned out," his mom added.

"You can't spend your life not doing things just because they make you feel uncomfortable," Dad said.

Ian butted into the conversation. He added, "You could pretend that you were somebody else when you were reading. You could pretend you were a scientist telling everyone about what you learned."

Normally, Zoltan would have been angry with his brother for butting in. However, in this case he seemed to have a good idea. If he just looked at the paper and pretended he was Foulke or Leidy or Cope it might not be so bad.

Also, he would be standing there right next to Haddy, or at least his statue. It would be as if he were William Foulke, back in 1858, standing in the Academy in Philadelphia with his new discovery.

"I'll do it," he announced. "Dad, you can make the copy for Mr. Giannotti. I'll read it in the Fall when Haddy's ready to go."

Epilogue

The sun was still warm on the day in October when Haddy took his place on Lantern Lane.

Two tons of bronze dinosaur was lifted up by a crane and placed on a truck at Mr. Giannotti's studio. Then Haddy, hidden under a big piece of cloth, was transported to the middle of town.

Crowds gathered by the roads as he passed. People wondered what the finished statue of the massive creature would look like.

In the center of town hundreds gathered and even a few television cameras appeared in the crowd. Zoltan was starting to get a sick and tingly feeling in his stomach. He was starting to think he couldn't do it after all.

The truck rolled up and he saw the huge blob that looked like a dinosaur ghost as it was once again lifted by crane and lowered into place.

The ghost of the Hadrosaurus foulkii came to rest just feet from where he stood. Cameras clicked and Zoltan's face felt hot. He was so nervous.

Then the mayor and the Garden Club people and Mr. Giannotti all came up to stand by the statue.

"This is indeed a great day for our little town of Haddonfield," the mayor said. "Today we mark the 145th anniversary of the finding of the world's most complete dinosaur skeleton. It was the event that forever changed the way science looks at the dinosaur. It all started here, with this once great creature."

The mayor stepped aside to allow Mr. Giannotti to speak. He was no longer covered in clay. Instead he was wearing his best suit and a big smile. He looked even more nervous than Zoltan, if that was possible.

"Well, I am very grateful for being given the chance to bring Haddy to life for all of us," he said. His voice was shaking. He was really nervous. "So let's take a look. Heeeeeere's Haddy!"

He pulled a rope and the cloth fell away. There stood the great plant eating dinosaur. The sun shone on the head of the metal sculpture. It looked as if Haddy had a twinkle in his eye. Zoltan smiled. The whole town applauded.

Mr. Giannotti took a bow. Then he introduced Zoltan.

"Many, many children have visited my studio over the past months while I worked on Haddy. I have had many letters, cards and pictures sent to me by school children from all over the area," he said.

"My neighbor Zoltan, has a poem I would like him to read it for all of you now."

Zoltan stepped up to the stage. Mr. Giannotti patted him on the shoulder. He whispered," Just look at Haddy and read it to him."

Zoltan looked up at the dinosaur and saw his eyes sparkling with life. He thought about how Foulke must have felt the first time he ever saw the skeleton standing there beside him. He wondered how he would have felt to see the sculpture with flesh and muscle all added to it.

Imagining this, he didn't feel scared anymore. He took a deep breath and read his poem.

It seemed to take forever as he read and read. Everyone was so quiet, he wondered if they liked it or not. But before he knew it he was reading the last words. "…it must be really big."

The crowd laughed and cheered and applauded. In front of the stage his parents, Ian and Avery all clapped and cheered.

He had done it. He had overcome his fear of being able to write the poem. He had been able to get up in front of everyone and read his poem.

Zoltan got off the stage and joined his family in the crowd.

"Excellent job!" his Dad said.

"I'm so proud," his mother said and wiped away a tear. "I always cry at epic poetry readings," she sniffed.

"Man, you did great," Ian said and gave him a hug."

Avery jumped up and down and yelled, "We had a Haddy! We had a Haddy!"

Mr. Giannotti came up and patted Zoltan on the shoulder again, "Well I'm glad that's over."

He looked at Zoltan's parents and added, "How about if we all go back to my studio and have some burgers. I sculpted them all into dinosaur shapes."

"Sounds delicious," Mom said. "After that we can head to our place for hadrosaurus sundaes. I buried candy bones under chocolate ice cream. We can excavate them until we get as fat as a stegosaurus!"

Zoltan grinned and shouted, "Sweet!"